The Shape Family Babies

by Kristin Haas

illustrated by Shennen Bersani

Once upon a time, a rectangle
and a rhombus fell in love.
They married and soon were
expecting their first child.

Each parent wondered whom the baby would look like.

Would the baby have four equal sides like Mother Rhombus?

Would the baby have four right angles like Father Rectangle?

They waited and waited. Finally the day arrived, and there was not one, not two, but three beautiful children.

The first had all equal sides like Mother Rhombus, and she was named Rhombus Jr.

The second had four right angles like Father Rectangle, and he was named Rectangle Jr.

The third was a bit of a surprise; she looked like both of her parents. She had four right angles *and* four equal sides.

What could they name this beautiful child?
Her parents decided to ask their relatives for ideas.

Cousin Triangle noted, "She has all straight sides connected end to end. We could name her Polygon."

Cousin Trapezoid suggested, "She has two sets of parallel sides. Why not name her Parallelogram?"

Aunt Hexagon proposed, "She has four angles. We could name her Quadrangle."

Uncle Pentagon recommended, "She has four sides. Why not name her Quadrilateral?"

Grandpa Rectangle reasoned, "She's a rectangle and a rhombus combined. We could name her Rectombus."

"*Pish posh*," scoffed Grandma Rhombus. "Who ever heard of a rectombus? Anyone can see she's a rhombus and a rectangle combined. We could just as well make up the name Rhombangle."

Her parents didn't know what to do.
They seemed to be getting nowhere fast
. . . until Great-Aunt Octagon arrived.

When she saw the little girl, Great-Aunt Octagon knew at once.

"Why, she's the spitting image of Great-Great-Grandpa Square. If she has four right angles and four equal sides, she's a square!"

It was agreed. Rhombus and Rectangle's youngest child would be called Square.

Square

For Creative Minds

Shape Parts

All of the shapes in this book are polygons. Polygons are two-dimensional shapes. They have length and width, but no height. Polygons are made of straight lines and angles. Polygons are closed shapes—each line ends where another begins.

When all of the angles are equal and all of the sides are the same length, it is called a **regular** shape.

If the angles are different and the sides are uneven, the shape is **irregular**.

There are three basic kinds of angles. If the angle measures exactly 90°, it is a **right** angle. If the angle is less than 90°, it is an **acute** angle. If it is more than 90°, it is an **obtuse** angle.

Angles are measured with a tool called a **protractor**.

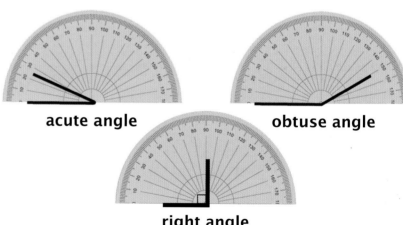

acute angle

obtuse angle

right angle

When two lines meet at a right angle, the lines are called **perpendicular**.

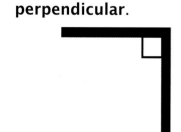

Sometimes lines in a shape are **parallel**. Parallel lines are always the same distance apart. They never touch and they never get closer to or farther away from each other.

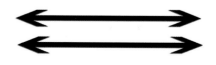

Quadrilaterals

A polygon with four lines is called a quadrilateral.
A polygon with four angles is called a quadrangle.

A quadrangle with exactly one pair of parallel sides is called a trapezoid. A trapezoid is a kind of polygon, a quadrilateral, and a quadrangle.

A quadrilateral that has two pairs of parallel sides is a parallelogram. A parallelogram is a type of polygon, a quadrilateral, and a quadrangle.

A parallelogram with all equal sides is a rhombus. A rhombus is a type of polygon, a quadrilateral, a quadrangle, and a parallelogram.

A parallelogram with all right angles is called a rectangle. A rectangle is a kind of polygon, a quadrilateral, a quadrangle, and a parallelogram.

A quadrilateral with all equal sides and all right angles is a square. A square is a certain type of polygon, a quadrilateral, a quadrangle, a parallelogram, a rhombus and a rectangle.

Name that Shape!

Match the description to the shape.

Pentagon

Hexagon

1. This shape is made of six lines that meet to create six angles.

2. Four right angles and four straight lines make this shape. The four sides can be all equal length or it can have two pairs of lines that are different lengths.

3. This shape has five sides.

4. This shape has four sides. It has one pair of parallel sides, but its other two sides are not parallel.

Trapezoid

Rectangle

Answers: 1-hexagon, 2-rectangle, 3-pentagon, 4-trapezoid

5. This four-sided shape is a parallelogram made of two pairs of parallel lines. All sides are the same length. The angles can be all right angles, but they don't have to be.

6. Eight sides join together to create this shape.

7. This shape is a kind of rectangle. It has four equal sides and four right angles. It is also a kind of rhombus. Each of the sides is parallel to another side.

8. This shape is made of three angles and three lines.

Triangle

Octagon

Rhombus

Square

To "squares" like me who know that math can be fun.—KH

To David Brewster who guided all four of my children with his dedication to teaching.—SB

Thanks to Rachel Hilchey, elementary math teacher with Hallsville ISD (TX), for verifying the accuracy of the information in this book.

Library of Congress Cataloging-in-Publication Data

Haas, Kristin, 1964-
  The shape family babies / by Kristin Haas ; illustrated by Shennen Bersani.
     pages cm
  Audience: Age 4-8.
  ISBN 978-1-62855-211-9 (English hardcover) -- ISBN 978-1-62855-220-1 (English pbk.) -- ISBN 978-1-62855-229-4 (Spanish pbk.) -- ISBN (invalid) 978-1-62855-238-6 (English ebook downloadable) -- ISBN 978-1-62855-247-8 (Spanish ebook downloadable) -- ISBN 978-1-62855-256-0 (English ebook dual language enhanced) -- ISBN 978-1-62855-265-2 (Spanish ebook dual language enhanced) 1. Shapes--Juvenile literature. 2. Names, Personal--Juvenile literature. I. Bersani, Shennen, illustrator. II. Title.
  QA445.5.H375 2014
  516'.15--dc23
                              2013044817

Also available in Spanish as *Los bebés de la familia geométrica*.

Lexile® Level: 580
key phrases for educators: anthropomorphic, classification, geometry, hereditary, individual differences, math, vocabulary

Text Copyright 2014 © by Kristin Haas
Illustration Copyright 2014 © by Shennen Bersani

Manufactured in China, December 2013
This product conforms to CPSIA 2008
First Printing

Sylvan Dell Publishing
Mt. Pleasant, SC 29464
www.SylvanDellPublishing.com